Jan 22

Here is a list of things people have said about Nina Soni.

"Nina Soni is many things: Indian American, a list-maker, a word-definer, and a big sister. She is funny, observant, and smart, and she can also sometimes be a bit forgetful. The number one thing that Nina is? Loveable! I adore Nina and know readers will, too."
—Debbi Michiko Florence, author of the *Jasmine Toguchi* series

"A perfect fit for readers who enjoy realistic fiction about friendship and self-discovery."
—*School Library Journal*

"...a flawed but refreshing and very likable protagonist..."
—*Booklist*

"A sweet and entertaining series opener about family and friendship."
—*Kirkus Reviews*

She's a phenomenon!

Phe-no-me-non means a happening or an event.

For Lucia, Ishan, Neha, and Karl, with love
—K. S.

Published by
PEACHTREE PUBLISHING COMPANY INC.
1700 Chattahoochee Avenue
Atlanta, Georgia 30318-2112
www.peachtree-online.com

Text © 2021 by Kashmira Sheth
Illustrations © 2021 by Jenn Kocsmiersky

Edited by Kathy Landwehr
Design and composition by Adela Pons
The illustrations were rendered digitally.

Printed in June 2021 by Lake Book Manufacturing in Melrose Park, Illinois, in the United States of America
10 9 8 7 6 5 4 3 2 1 (hardcover)
10 9 8 7 6 5 4 3 2 1 (trade paperback)
First Edition
HC ISBN 978-1-68263-227-7
PB ISBN 978-1-68263-228-4

Cataloging-in-Publication Data is available from the Library of Congress.

NINA SONI
HALLOWEEN QUEEN

Written by **Kashmira Sheth**
Illustrated by **Jenn Kocsmiersky**

PEACHTREE
ATLANTA

CHAPTER ONE

Every year I am set for Halloween long before it arrives. I always know what I am going to dress up as and I keep my costume ready. In the evening, I go out trick or treating with my little sister Kavita and my best friend Jay.

Not this year though.

It was already Friday and Halloween was on Sunday.

On my way to school, I wondered why I was not prepared for Halloween this year. Maybe I should make a list of reasons. I love making lists.

I even have a notebook where I write them down. I have named it Sakhi.

Sakhi means friend in Hindi.

Sakhi is not a diary, because I don't write long letters to her. It's a tell-everything-quick kind of notebook.

Reasons why I like Sakhi

* She has a great memory. She remembers everything I have ever told her.
* If I forget what I have told Sakhi, I can go back to her.
* I never worry about our friendship.
* She never spills my secrets.
* Sakhi always has time for me.

Since I was walking to school with Kavita and Jay, I couldn't write down my list. That didn't stop me from making one though.

In-my-head list of why I was not ready for Halloween

* I did start thinking about Halloween three weeks ago.

* But then my brain changed from its Halloween track to its Diwali track. That was because this year Diwali fell on Thursday, three days before Halloween.

* We celebrate Diwali (even though now our family lives in the United States) just like Mom and Dad did when they were growing up in India. We hang twinkling lights on our trees in the front yard. We decorate our home with gleaming copper and brass lamps and bright embroidered tablecloths, placemats, and other things. We get new clothes to wear; we eat delicious food, and we light

fireworks and spend time with our family and friends.

* So for the last two weeks, I was busy with Diwali preparation and celebration.

* On Diwali day, my sister Kavita and I took the day off from school. We talked to my grandparents and cousin Montu in India. We helped Mom and Dad prepare pastries filled with nuts and homemade cheese. In the evening, Jay and his parents came over. We had a delicious meal and then Jay, Kavita, and I lit some sparklers. It was fun.

* Now Diwali was over and I remembered Halloween.

What was I going to dress up as? I didn't have enough time to order a costume from the internet. Nothing would be left in the stores. I wondered if Mom and Dad had bought any candy.

Jay and Kavita probably hadn't forgotten about Halloween. They were walking in front of me, busy talking. Maybe about their costumes? All of a sudden, I was right smack in the middle of their conversation.

Con-ver-sa-tion means to talk about something. Anything.

Jay: "We only use 10 percent of our brains."

Kavita: "I use all of mine."

Jay: "That can't be true. No one can use 100 percent of their brain."

Kavita: "Who says that?"

Jay: "The scientists who study human brains."

Kavita: "Even *they* can only use 10 percent of their brains?"

Jay: "Yes."

Kavita: "Well, I don't believe them. I use 100 percent of my brain. So I believe myself."

Then she covered her ears and sang, "*La-dee-da-dee-da*." That meant their conversation was finished.

By then, we were at school. The first bell had already rung and the playground was empty.

"See you later, Nina," Jay said and went toward our fourth-grade classroom.

I took Kavita to her first-grade class, then rushed to mine.

When I walked in, Jay was already at his desk, writing furiously in his notebook. I wondered what that was about.

I tried to peek as I walked past Jay.

He looked up, smiled, and covered part of the notebook with his hand. That made me even more curious.

Was he writing about his and Kavita's conversation?

It certainly wasn't a list. Jay is not a list-making, organized kind of person. He is more of a mix-it-all-up, doodle kind of person. So what was he writing about? Or was he doodling?

I sat at my desk and turned away from Jay to face Ms. Lapin. She was writing on the whiteboard.

"Nina," he whispered.

My idea worked. When I paid no attention to him, he called to me.

I didn't answer. It is very hard to pretend to pay no attention to someone when you are actually paying *all* your attention.

"Hey! Nina!" Jay whispered again.

I looked at him. "What?"

"Did you finish the social studies homework? It's due today."

"I finished it the day we got it," I told him.

"Of course you did."

"What's that supposed to mean?"

"Nothing," he said. "You always get stuff done before you need to. Except when you forget. And you forget a lot."

It was true. And I knew that. I folded my arms. "Fine."

That Jay! One annoying thing about someone being your best friend is that they know most everything about you. Not fair.

Mom says I forget things, because I have too many ideas in my head going this way and that way. But if that's true, then won't they create an idea jam? If that happened, then none of the ideas would be able to go anyplace. But my ideas always have places to go, so I don't think they ever got jammed up.

Here is how my brain works. I think and think about something, but when a new thing comes up, I jump to a different track. That's when the first idea gets lost. Like Halloween did.

If we use only 10 percent of our brains, I wonder how many unused tracks there are in mine? If they all started working, what would I do? How would I keep them going?

Right now I should not worry about more ideas. I should think about my Halloween costume.

Jay leaned closer. "You're thinking of something else. You already forgot about our conversation!"

"I did not." Just as I turned away from Jay I thought of something. I turned right back. "Were you finishing your homework now?"

"No. That was not homework."

The bell rang. I waited for him to say what it was after the bell finished ringing, but he was silent.

"What were you working on?" I whispered.

Jay's green eyes twinkled like shiny new marbles. "I designed my own Halloween costume. My mom made it for me. I was adding some details to it."

I gasped. "What is it?"

"It's a secret. You'll see it on Halloween, when I have it on."

Best friends don't keep their Halloween costume secret from each other. Do they?

Jay's mom, Meera Masi, was good with thread, needles, and a sewing machine. She could make anything Jay wanted.

Even though Jay and I are best friends, we like to compete. That's probably why he was keeping his costume a secret. I wondered what he had planned. I didn't want him to have the best Halloween costume while I was costume-less. I should be someone grand and important.

"What are you going to be?" Jay asked.

"Halloween Queen," I blurted out.

"Wow!" Jay was impressed. "What does your costume look like?"

"You'll see," I said. I was worried though.

Halloween was on Sunday. With so little time left, a store-bought queen costume was my only choice. A flimsy, plasticky outfit, because unlike Meera Masi, Mom can't sew.

Once I begged her to make me a dress. We bought a pattern, material, thread, and a zipper. When the dress was done, she asked me to try it on. But the zipper was inside-out. In order to zip it up, I had to stick my hand between my back and my dress, and try to pull it up from the inside. That was not an easy thing to do.

And the dress was tight on one side and loose on the other. I looked like a melting, lopsided ice cream cone.

That was the last time Mom ever tried to sew. After that I never asked her to sew anything again, and I don't think she wanted to either. Another time I asked Dad to sew a button and it took him fifteen minutes. And then next day it came off. So this weekend it was better to let Mom do fall garden cleanup and Dad rake leaves. They were good at that and happy doing it.

For the rest of the day, I kept thinking. I made an in-my-head list of possibilities.

* Neither Mom nor Dad could sew. So I couldn't ask them to make a queen costume.

* Maybe I could get a magical pumpkin. Then the pumpkin could turn into a beautiful queen's robe.

* That was not possible. The pumpkin idea was a dumbkin idea.

* I could decorate our yard and turn it into a Halloween palace. But I would still be without a costume.

* And it is always dark when trick or treaters came, so no one would notice all my work.

* No good ideas here.

It is frustrating when you have so many ideas in your head and yet you can't come up with one that will beat all the others.

At lunch I talked to my friend Megan. She is not in my class so we only see each other at lunch.

"What are you going to be for Halloween?" I asked.

"I told you three days ago," she said. "You were not paying attention."

"I'm sorry." I offered one of the Diwali pastries I had brought.

"Thanks," she said. "I'm going to be a cowgirl. I have a big hat and fancy boots and everything ready." She took a bite of pastry.

"That sounds great." I was happy for Megan, but I felt miserable.

"This is delicious," she said taking another bite. "What are you going to be?"

"I told Jay I am going to be the Halloween Queen. The only problem is I have no costume and no idea how I can get one."

"You can borrow my tiara," she said.

"Thanks! But how can I get the rest of the costume ready in two days?" I asked. "Forty-eight hours?"

"Nina, make a list and write down your ideas. I'm sure you can come up with something."

Megan was right. I could do it. I *had* to do something special. Something dazzling. As a queen, I needed to own this holiday. I needed to reign over the holiday. Like a real queen. A queen everyone had to listen to. A queen who was regal, brilliant, and definitely extraordinary.

Ex-traor-di-nary means something extra is thrown in, so it's way more than ordinary.

The more I thought about it, the more I got excited about the idea.

Nina Soni, Halloween Queen!

I had to find a way to become one.

CHAPTER TWO

Kavita ran up the driveway when we got home from school, but I stopped at the mailbox. It was filled with catalogs for Mom, who is a landscape architect. That means she's a garden and plant person. By the end of October nothing grows in Wisconsin except for darkness, winter jackets, mittens, and hats. So it was nice to see a lot of colorful flowers and plants in our mailbox.

I scooped up all the mail, slid in the door Kavita had left open, and handed the pile to Mom. Then we had our snack and I went upstairs to my room.

Even though I wanted to talk to Mom about being the Halloween Queen, I decided to do my homework first. That way I would have the rest of the weekend free. Or maybe it was because Mom always wants me to do my homework first. (That way I don't forget to do it.) Anyway, most of the time, it is a good idea. By the time I was finished studying, it was as dark as a doorknob.

Sometimes, doorknobs are not dark. Many are shiny silver or gold colored. But I like saying "as dark as a doorknob." It is soothing to my ears.

Kavita was singing. I couldn't hear the words. Whatever it was, it wasn't soothing.

As dark as a doorknob is much more soothing than her singing. Kavita means "poetry" in Hindi, so I guess it is not her fault that she likes to make up poetry and sings.

Maybe things would be different if Mom and Dad had named Kavita something else. Like Chitra. Chitra means "drawing" in Hindi, so maybe she would sit in a corner and draw. Sapna would also be a good name. It means "dream" in Hindi. Then she might dream and dream.

But she is Kavita, so she makes up poetry and sings and sings.

Nina means "beautiful eyes." What can you do with beautiful eyes? Maybe stare? It was dark outside and I could not see anything. I was stuck with doing nothing. The only thing I could do was to open and close my eyes and look around my room.

Boring!

Then I remembered! I had to work on finding, inventing, or making my costume.

I rushed downstairs.

Kavita was at the dining room table, coloring and singing. *"If I surprise you silly, don't be a whiny. Just sing along with me, and be in my liney!"*

I have no idea what "liney" means. It rhymes with "whiny," so I guess that was good enough for Miss Poetry.

"What are you coloring?" I asked.

"It is a monarch butterfly. It is orange and black, just like my Halloween costume."

I walked over to her. "There's no way Mom can make you this costume," I said. "She can't sew."

Kavita looked up at me. "Mom doesn't even know about my costume. Meera Masi said she would make me whatever I wanted."

That's the last thing I needed to hear. Meera Masi was making costumes for both Kavita and Jay. Why hadn't I thought of asking? Now it was too late.

I wished I could open and close my ears instead of my beautiful eyes. That way I could have shut out Kavita's singing, *"If I surprise you silly, don't be a whiny."* Then I wouldn't have gone to see what she was doing and found out about her costume. Now I knew that everyone else would have something wonderful to wear except me.

I was miserable.

Double miserable.

Triple miserable.

Maybe it wouldn't be a big deal. Last year it was so cold on Halloween that we had to bundle up in our jackets and scarves. This Sunday was going to be warm though. That meant everyone would see our costumes.

Maybe I could wear my langha outfit. It had a beautiful skirt and cropped top with a matching scarf. But I had worn it yesterday for Diwali. And a cropped-top outfit is not a good idea for trick or treating in Madison, Wisconsin. No matter how warm they say it is going to be, I would freeze.

I had to think of something that would be truly queenly. Something that would keep me warm.

I was an idea person. Maybe I needed to use more than 10 percent of my brain to come up with an idea.

I took out Sakhi to write down my thoughts.

A list of what Halloweens is all about

* Halloween is a dress-up holiday, but I don't have a special costume and Kavita and Jay do.

* Halloween is an orange-and-black holiday.

Kavita's monarch butterfly colors are perfect for Halloween.

* Halloween is a trick-or-treat holiday. Maybe I could trick people. When they knock, maybe I could play scary music. But maybe not. Because I will be out trick or treating myself.

* Halloween is a scary holiday. How could I scare people? I could build a haunted house!

I might not have an amazing costume, but a haunted house would be special. If I was going to be a queen I should make it a haunted palace. I could charge kids to visit it. That way I could make money, have fun, and scare the visitors. I could be a real Halloween Queen.

I opened a brand-new page of Sakhi, and wrote down a new list:

What I need for a Halloween haunted palace
✳ A dark place
✳ Building material
✳ Scary, slimy, gooey, gross stuff
✳ Haunted music
✳ ~~Nasty smell~~

I crossed out the last one. No one wants to smell nasty stuff. I certainly don't want to, so I wouldn't have any in my haunted palace.

Once my list was done, I looked for the perfect location for my haunted palace.

The backyard was the biggest place. I turned on the porch light and went outside with Sakhi. It was spooky all right, with darkness and trees and wind, but what if it turned cold or rained? No one would visit my haunted palace.

My haunted palace needed to be scary and dark but

also warm and comfortable. That way I could get all the neighborhood kids to visit it.

I had to build it inside the house.

My room was a possibility, but it had a few disadvantages.

Dis–ad–van–tages means there are some problems with something.

Here are the disadvantages of using my room to build a haunted palace.

* I had to clean it up first.

* Even if I did clean up, it would be too small unless I could also use my bed.

* But then where would I sleep for the next few days? As much as I liked the idea of a haunted palace, I didn't want to sleep in a haunted bed.

I walked from room to room. Kavita's room is smaller than mine, so it wouldn't work. Mom and Dad's room would be the best place.

"Mom, do you like Halloween?" I asked. She was folding clothes in her room.

"Sure," she said. "It is a fun holiday."

I folded a napkin. "You like being spooked and scared?"

"Sure do."

I think the word "sure" was stuck in Mom's head. Which was good. Maybe I could make her say "sure" again.

"How would you like it if I turned your room into a haunted palace?" I asked. "I'll do all the work. Would you like that?"

I waited to catch the "sure," when it tumbled out of Mom's mouth. But it did not.

A crisp, no-nonsense "no!" came out instead. She didn't even say, "No thanks, I don't want our room to turn into a haunted palace" or "It is very nice of you to offer that, but I don't think so." It was just plain "No!"

I didn't even try to convince Dad to convert their room into the haunted palace.

Then a bright idea flashed in my head.

The basement!

I scribbled my thoughts down in Sakhi.

The basement is the best place to build a haunted palace because

* It is dark even during the daytime.

* It has its own smell. It is not stinky, but it doesn't smell sunshiny and flowery.

* It's big enough to hold a haunted palace.

* No one sleeps there. That means no one has to sleep in a haunted bed.

* It's in the house, so it would be warm and dry for visitors.

I went downstairs to check it out. I sniffed. It still had the "basement smell" I remembered.

There are three rooms in our basement.

I made a quick in-my-head list.

* One room is carpeted and heated. It is too nice to be a haunted palace.
* The second has the furnace, water heater, washer, dryer, and stuff like that. Mom and Dad wouldn't let me build a haunted palace in there.
* The third is full of all the boxes that we have not recycled yet.

The third room was huge and pretty clean except for the boxes. There were big boxes from the washer and dryer and a gigantic one from the refrigerator. If I wanted to use the room for my haunted palace, I would have to clean up the boxes first.

"Kavita," I called up the stairs, "do you want to help me with a special project?"

She came down right away. But instead of helping, she wiggled inside a box. When I called her again, she popped out like a jack-in-the-box.

"Did I scare you?" she asked.

"No, you did not. Now can you help me carry these boxes upstairs?"

"I want to keep them here," she whined. "It is fun to play with them."

This was not going to work. Kavita wanted to play with the boxes and I wanted to get rid of them.

As Jack—I mean Kavita—popped in and out of the box, a new idea began to roll along my brain track.

I could use the boxes as building material for my haunted palace.

I smiled. It was good that Mom and Dad had not cut them up and recycled them.

I went back upstairs. Kavita followed me. She watched me.

I opened Sakhi and updated my list.

✱	A dark place ✓
✱	Building material ✓
✱	Scary, slimy, gooey, gross stuff—not yet

✳ Haunted music—very possible

✳ ~~Nasty smell? Musty smell?~~

"Does our basement smell musty to you?" I asked Kavita.

"Not musty, not rusty, maybe a little dusty," she said.

"OK."

I put a slash through the last item.

Now I needed some tape and scissors and markers and stuff like that. That was the easiest part. All I had to do was to ask Kavita if I could borrow her art supplies. She may not be Chitra the artist, but she has a lot of art supplies.

"Kavita, do you want to help me make a haunted palace?"

Her eyes turned into two coins, round and shiny. "Sure."

"We'll need your art supplies."

"Why do we have to use my stuff?"

"Because by fourth grade you don't have that many art supplies anymore."

"What if I don't want to use my stuff?"

"If you want to be part of the haunted palace, you have to contribute."

"What is 'contribute'?"

"Contribute means you have to give something to make it happen."

Kavita folded her arms. "You're giving nothing."

"I am too. It is my idea," I said. "And I will do a lot of the work."

Kavita stomped her foot. "An idea is not something."

"An idea is everything."

"If you have everything then why do you need my art supplies?"

I was stuck. We could keep arguing forever about something, nothing, and everything. I was thinking about what I should do to avoid this when Mom came in with laundry.

"What are you two arguing about?"

"I am building a haunted palace in here. I'm going to

have all the neighborhood kids visit. I told Kavita if she wants to help me, she must contribute something. Like her art supplies."

"But Nina is not contributing anything," Kavita said. "That's not fair."

"But it is my idea, and the idea is the most important thing. Isn't it, Mom?"

"Nina, your idea is important, but there is another important thing that you are missing. It is called 'permission.' You have not asked your dad or me for permission to build a haunted palace and invite the neighborhood kids."

I wished I could say, "I *have* asked Dad," but I had not.

How could I have forgotten? I mean, I have been a kid all my life. I should have known that without permission, my palace was not possible.

> Per-mis-sion is something like having a password. Kids need permission to do things.

"Mom, could I please build a haunted palace in our basement?"

I held my breath.

CHAPTER THREE

I didn't have to hold my breath too long, because Mom said, "I suppose the basement is a better place to build a haunted palace than our bedroom. What do you have in mind? I certainly don't want a mess. And don't use the carpeted area."

Another important thing to remember if you are a kid is that your parents don't have to say yes or no to your idea. They can keep on talking about it until your idea fades away. One way I keep my ideas alive is to make a list in Sakhi or even in my head. It really helps.

"It won't be a mess. It will just be a Halloween palace."
I didn't say "slimy, gooey, and gross," because I was sure
Mom would think that would be messy.

"What will you use to make your palace?" Mom
sounded like one of her clients when they asked what kinds
of shrubs and trees she was planning to plant in their yard.

I answered just the way she does. "I will use whatever
works best for the space and our climate."

Her eyebrows went up, but then her eyes twinkled. "I
see."

I didn't want Mom to say "I see." I wanted her to say yes.

"Please, Mom. I won't make a mess and I will clean up
everything at the end."

"OK," she said. "Make sure you include your sister."

"Only if she contributes her art supplies."

"Do I have to?" Kavita asked. "Nina only has ideas and
I have to give everything."

"Not everything. Just the use of your art supplies,"
Mom said.

"And only if you want to be part of it," I added, hoping Kavita wouldn't back out.

"O...kay," Kavita said.

Mom squeezed my shoulder. "You are a great sister," she said before she left to do the laundry.

That compliment made me dancing happy.

"Kavita, let's start," I said.

"Why are we making it in the basement?" Kavita asked.

"The basement is the best place. It is already a little spooky, right?"

"No, it's not. You tumble and fumble in the dark, but when you turn on the light, everything is fine."

"But without light it is a little scary, right?"

She didn't answer.

If I couldn't scare Kavita with my haunted palace idea, who could I scare? She is three years younger than me, so she should get scared much faster than me. But then Kavita has never been very scared of the dark. She actually likes darkness. Maybe other kids in our neighborhood are not so darkness-friendly.

I'd have to keep my fingers crossed. "Kavita, let's use these boxes as our building material."

She walked right into the big refrigerator box, but I was too tall for that.

Then she slipped sideways into the washing machine box. "Can you put this right side up?" she asked.

"I can't lift it with you in there." I told her. "The box will probably break."

"How are we going to build a haunted palace for people to go through using boxes that would break?"

Kavita was right.

If I couldn't fit in the box, how would other kids walk through it? We couldn't build a haunted palace with cardboard boxes, because they couldn't stand up in them.

"What are we going to do?" she asked as she crawled out of the box like an earthworm in spring—head sticking out, body still buried in the soil. Well, not really soil, but a brown box. It was the color of soil.

That gave me another idea. A palace was not possible but something else was.

"Kavita, what if we build a haunted tunnel? Kids will have to slide and crawl through the tunnel, but that would be part of the fun. Right?"

"Like the way I just did?"

"Yup. We have to connect the boxes, so we have a long, twisty tunnel."

We arranged all the empty boxes by size from big to small. Then we moved them around and mixed them up. We made the tall refrigerator box our entrance.

Behind it, we placed a short box that once held a pair of lawn flamingoes. I know that because it had a picture of a flamingo on the top. One of Mom's clients wanted a pair of flamingos, but she didn't want pink plastic ones like they have on the University of Wisconsin lawn. She said they looked cheap. So she asked Mom to get her sturdy brass ones. I knew all about it, because Mom had talked about it for days.

Anyway, when you crawled into the refrigerator box you could be as wide as you wanted to be. Then you had to become as skinny as a pair of flamingos and squeeze through the next part of the tunnel. I liked how a person would have to crawl and then suddenly creep.

After that we put the washer box, and then a box that had come from India full of spices. Kids were probably going to sneeze when they were in that part of the tunnel.

Kavita sneezed four times and I sneezed twice, and we didn't even go in the box.

Once we had the boxes in place, our tunnel circled the room. But it wasn't really a tunnel. Not yet.

I didn't realize that the easiest part was done. We had arranged our boxes. Now was the difficult part. Next we would need to open up the ends of the boxes.

I wished Jay was here. Kavita was a good helper, but someone like Jay could really help me cut the boxes or flatten the flaps. I thought about calling him, but then he would know what I was doing for Halloween. He wouldn't tell me about his costume, so I felt like it was better to keep my haunted palace idea a secret from him.

Like I told Kavita, ideas are the most important thing and I couldn't just give this idea away.

Even to my best friend.

✳✳✳

On Saturday morning right after breakfast, Kavita and I went downstairs. I began cutting the boxes. But the scissors were too small and hurt my hand.

"Get the big scissors, like Mom uses in the kitchen, Kavita," I said.

She didn't say anything and didn't move.

"Kavita, if you want to help, you have to do what I say."

"You didn't say 'please.'" Kavita shook her head. "You are not the boss."

I had a quick reply for that. "No, but I am the boss of the Halloween Tunnel. I'm the Halloween Queen."

Her face fell but then lighted up again. "I'm not allowed to touch the big scissors. That is why I can't get them for you."

I guess she was right, but it still annoyed me.

An-noyed means you are opposite of happy.

"OK. I will get them," I said and went upstairs.

I knew I wasn't allowed to use the kitchen scissors to cut paper, but I guessed I could use them to cut boxes.

Here are my reasons why I thought I could use the special kitchen scissors to cut boxes.

* Boxes are not paper. I mean, nobody would look at a box and say, "That paper is huge."
* Also, mostly we were cutting the tape that was holding the bottom of the boxes together. No one would call a piece of tape paper.
* So I thought it was OK to use the scissors.

I took them downstairs.

Even using the sharp kitchen scissors, it was a lot of work to cut everything, but I finally did it. Kavita was not allowed to use those scissors, so she couldn't help me.

As soon as I was done, Kavita held her art bucket full of markers, crayons, and colored pencils. She announced,

"Now it's time to decorate the tunnel with butterflies and flowers."

"Not butterflies and flowers! Only spiders and ghosts," I said.

"Everybody decorates with ghosts and goblins and icky stuff for Halloween. Why can't we do ours differently? Isn't it nice to have something that nobody else has?"

She kind of had a point there. But butterflies and flowers on Halloween?

"No. This is not a secret garden."

Kavita stormed upstairs with her art supplies. I followed her.

"Stop! Maybe we could do some of both."

But she didn't stop.

✳✳✳

Usually, the best way to make Kavita come running back to me was to ignore her. I know my sister. If I ignored her, but I still talked about my haunted tunnel, she would want to be part of it again. Plus, her idea of drawing butterflies and flowers on the outside was not so bad. Even a haunted tunnel can have a garden.

Kavita was arranging her crayons on the dining table. She wasn't singing. It was my chance to speak.

"Mom, will you lend me some of your old scarves and saris for *my* haunted tunnel?" I asked, making "my" sound strong and big.

Kavita stopped arranging her crayons. She was listening.

"I just cleaned out my closet and put the old stuff in a bag in my room. I suppose I can give you a few things from that," Mom said.

"Thanks. And may I use your old flower catalogs and garden magazines? I can cut pictures and stick them on *my* boxes."

This time I made "my" sound playful and sweet.

Kavita looked at me.

"Excellent idea," Mom said.

"I think my haunted tunnel is going to be great." This time I didn't make "my" strong or sweet.

Mom's eyes darted between Kavita and me. "I thought both you and Kavita were working on it."

I sighed. "We were, but she changed her mind. It's OK. I can do it myself."

Kavita stomped her foot. "I want to do it too."

"OK," I said, as quick as a carriage. A carriage is only as quick as the horse it is hitched to. But "as quick as a carriage" sounds better than "as quick as a horse." I know all about horses and carriages because Megan's uncle owns a farm, cows, horses, and two carriages.

Mom smiled, Kavita looked ready to help and I was happy.

Mom went to her room and came down with two saris and several dupattas. I took the saris and Kavita took the scarves.

"Thanks, Mom," I said.

"Now we can finally decorate the tunnel," Kavita said.

"Let's make a list of ideas first," I suggested. "It's good to have a plan."

"You're full of ideas and plans, just like I am full of songs and singing. Nina, let's just do it."

Sometimes my sister makes sense. "OK," I said.

CHAPTER FOUR

We took the saris and scarves downstairs.

Kavita had said I didn't need a list. I had agreed with her. But now my head started making one anyway.

In-my-head list of what I needed to do
✳ Clear the space around the tunnel.
✳ Decorate the tunnel.
✳ Make the inside scary.
✳ Make the invitations.
✳ Deliver the invitations.

Kavita and I took out the boxes we weren't going to use.

"Now we can really see the tunnel," I said.

"Let's make it pretty," Kavita said.

My idea and her idea about the tunnel were not the same. If Jay were here he would understand why I wanted to make it haunted. I missed him.

"Come on, Nina," Kavita said. She was already decorating the outside of the refrigerator box.

"Let's decorate each box separately. That way it will be easy," I said. "Then we will put the tunnel back together."

I worked on the inside of the refrigerator box. Each of us kept peeking at what other one was doing.

"Decorating this box is the best part of making the tunnel," Kavita said.

"Wait until we do other things to make the tunnel scary. That's going to be real fun."

Kavita sang, *"Fun, fun, scary for some. Sun, sun, scary for worms."*

I didn't ask her what she meant by sun being scary for worm. Sometimes it's best to let Kavita make up songs and sing it. That way she was happy and I was getting our tunnel-making work done.

She drew butterflies and flowers and even wiggly earthworms. I went with spiders, spiderwebs, and lizards. (I think lizards are creepier than spiders.) Next came the flamingo box and then the washer box. I decorated them with bats—flying bats, sleeping bats, and just hanging-out bats that I had cut from the *National Geographic* magazines and glued on the cardboard boxes.

I was so busy that I didn't know what Kavita was doing on the outside. When I finally checked on her, I dropped my last bat in surprise. She had turned the outside of the washer box into a giant ladybug. She had painted it red and put black spots on it. But what was most amazing was how she had created the two antennae from black pipe cleaners.

"This is awesome," I said.

"I know," Kavita replied.

Then something struck me. If everyone entered the haunted tunnel from the refrigerator door, then they wouldn't see the *outside* of the washer box—I mean the ladybug. They wouldn't see all the work Kavita had done.

If I told her that no one would see her artwork, she

would be upset. She would want to move her box so everyone could see it. But then what would happen to all my work? I stayed silent.

"Don't you think everyone will love my ladybug?" Kavita asked.

"Um…yes," Then I mumbled, "If they see it."

"What did you say?"

"Nothing."

"Yes, you did say something." She put her hands on her hips. She has learned this watching our neighbor, Mrs. Crump. Kavita looked funny with her hands on her hips, especially because she was still sitting on the floor. She looked so cute and sweet and not at all bossy like she was trying to be.

I sighed. Kavita is my sister and I know it's not good to hide things from her. So I told her, "If it's dark, they may not see the ladybug."

Her face fell like a crumpled leaf all ready to break into a hundred pieces.

She threw her hands up just like Mrs. Crump. "Then what are we going to do?"

"I don't know," I said.

"You're the idea person."

She had a point. And it was sharp and aimed in my direction.

The best way to avoid being poked by Kavita was to distract her. I stretched. My feet, arms, and back felt better. I knew my brain needed stretching too. "We have been in the basement too long," I said. "Taking a break will help me come up with an idea about how we can make your awesome ladybug visible."

"Isible? What's that?"

"*Visible*. It means that everyone can see it."

"I do want everyone to see my ladybug," she said.

"While we're thinking, we can make an invitation about our haunted tunnel to hand out to the neighbors."

"That's not taking a break."

"It is too. We're taking a break from decorating."

"The real break is when you do something fun. Like eat, sing, and dance," she said.

"You do that and I will work on the invitation."

"OK," she said.

When we went upstairs Kavita asked, "Mom, can I have some snack?"

"Sure. Have some pomegranate, I just opened one." Mom turned to me. "I am going out to work in the garden. Dad is raking leaves. Could you please keep an eye on Kavita?"

"I will," I said. "Is it OK if I print out our invitations?"

"Sure," Mom said.

As I worked alone on the invitation, I wished Jay were here. He could have helped me and he would have had some good ideas too. Being the only idea person can make your head feel heavy, like a stomach stuffed with an entire pizza. I wished Jay could have eaten some of the pizza slices—I mean, used some of his brain to work with me.

But I didn't have that choice. This was my project. I was the only idea person. Kavita was busy eating pomegranate.

Just when I had given up on ideas, one came by on a new track. That's how idea tracks in my brain work. I borrowed Mom's phone and took a picture of Kavita's ladybug, antennae and all.

Kavita was done eating and had moved on to singing and dancing. *"Halloween, Halloween, here you come, trick or treat, here we come."*

I showed the picture to her. "We'll put it on the invitation. Then everyone will see it."

Kavita stopped dancing and singing. "Wow!" Then she shook her head. "But no one will be able to see the real one."

"Maybe we'll figure out a way."

I pasted the picture in a document and then typed the words for my invitation.

On the bottom, I added a picture of a skeleton with flying bats hovering around it. I printed out twenty-five copies. The Halloween Queen was in business!

The Halloween Queen and this cute ladybug invite you to visit a Halloween tunnel!

But beware...
Come prepared to crawl, twist, turn,
and be scared.

Admission **$1.00** for kids under 12.
(If you are older than 12, you won't fit in the tunnel.)

Where: The tunnel of the Halloween Queen.
(It's in the basement of the Soni family's house)

When: 1:00–3:30 pm on Halloween

Please have your
Mom or Dad sign
this invitation and
bring it back with the
entrance fee.

By the time I was finished with the invitation, Kavita was finished eating, singing, and dancing.

We headed outside. I carried the stack of paper. Kavita took out her red scooter and helmet and I walked beside her on the sidewalk.

When I didn't stop at our next-door neighbor's house, Kavita hopped off her scooter. "Why are you skipping the Crumps' house?"

"Because they are older than twelve. They can't crawl through the tunnel."

"But Mrs. Crump is so tiny. I bet she can fit through the tunnel."

"But Mr. Crump can't. Let's go."

Kavita didn't move. "He can come to watch her go through the tunnel."

"I don't think so," I said.

"You are not the boss," Kavita said.

"I'm the queen of the tunnel."

She pointed. "Jay just went into his garage."

I was glad that seeing Jay had distracted her.

The air was fresh and light, but somehow it didn't do anything for my heavy mood. I figured I felt that way because I was missing Jay.

Should I ask Jay for help? I wondered. Maybe building the Halloween tunnel with him would be fun. Doing a project with a friend is always nice. The idea made my mood feel lighter.

Ever since Jay's two cousins moved from California to Wisconsin, he has been very busy on weekends. I wished my cousins could move here, but they live in India so I don't think that is going to happen. Jay's family is all around him; his Grandpa Joe, his aunt and uncle, and his cousins, Nora and Jeff.

Now Jay and Jeff came out of the garage with bikes. My lighter mood didn't feel so light anymore.

I worried that now Jay's best friend was Jeff, because they spent so much time together. Seeing them made both my brain and heart feel heavy at the same time.

Jay and Jeff were riding their bikes straight toward us. How could I avoid them?

It wasn't fair. Jay and I have been friends since before I even knew what friends were. I know how long we've been friends because I have seen so many of pictures of us: playing in a sandbox, eating watermelon slices at a picnic, giving each other hugs when we were two. I wouldn't want to give Jay a hug now, because now we are both fourth graders and fourth graders don't do those things.

Jay waved.

That made me feel better. I waved back.

Maybe Jeff was leaving. I crossed my fingers.

"Hi Jay," I said as he slowed down beside us. Jeff had already peddled by. I hid the invitations behind my back. "Do you want to build something with us?"

I reminded myself that I didn't want to give away my tunnel building idea, because ideas are the most important things you have. They are your intellectual stuff.

In-tel-lec-tu-al means it comes right out of your own brain.

My idea of the haunted tunnel had come from my own brain and I didn't want to share it with Jeff.

"What are you building?" Jay asked.

Jeff was a few feet ahead. He turned. "Come on, Jay!"

Kavita tapped Jay's handlebar. "What we're doing is way more fun than biking."

Jay looked confused. "But what is it, Nina? Something to do with you being a Halloween Queen?"

I wished I could cross my arms to show Jay I was not going to tell him. But I was still hiding the invitations behind my back. "I asked you a question first and you didn't answer. Do you want to build something with us?"

"First I want to know what you're building. I don't want to be Halloween Queen's servant."

"What are you going to be?" I asked.

"Not a servant for sure," Kavita piped in.

"Don't say a word more," Jay said to Kavita.

I wondered if Kavita knew what Jay was going to be. If she did, I was certain Jay didn't tell her about it. Maybe she asked Meera Masi and she told her. Anyway, Jay wasn't going to tell me what he had planned to be. Tomorrow was Halloween so why was he still keeping it a secret?

"Before I tell you anything, I want to know if you want to help us," I said.

"Hey, are you coming or not?" Jeff called. He sounded annoyed.

He certainly was making me annoyed.

Kavita put her arms up. "Let's not fight, kids."

She sounded just like Dad.

CHAPTER FIVE

We were silent. For a second.

And then Jeff biked back and got off. "This is that smart girl, right?"

"Jeff, we've met before," I said. "Don't you remember my name?"

I looked at Jay. He didn't say anything, but his face looked all red and kind of uncomfortable.

Un-com-fort-able means you wish you could be somewhere else, anywhere else, but where you are.

It was probably because

* Jay remembered Jeff and I had met.
* Or Jay must have talked to Jeff about the smart girl, me. (I kind of liked that.)
* Or both.

"I'm not that smart," I said, even though I am smart. I just didn't want to brag.

Kavita tugged my arm. "It's better to be smart than not smart."

"I know," I whispered.

"What are you hiding behind your back?" Jay asked.

"Nothing," I said.

Kavita said, "Invitations."

"For what?" Jay wanted to know.

Kavita looked at me but stayed quiet. I think she realized I didn't want to tell Jay.

He extended his hand. "Can I see?"

Jeff was smirking. I didn't like that.

I kept my hands behind my back. "You didn't want to tell me about your costume, Jay. Why would I let you see my invitations?"

He looked at me as if I had trapped him and he couldn't get out. "That's different," he said.

"Why is it different, Jay? We used to plan together what we were going to dress up as for Halloween. Now you want to keep it all a secret, and you still want me to tell you everything. It's not fair." I must have been upset because my words came out too fast.

Jay glanced at Jeff, so I did too.

Jeff was smirking. Again.

Jay tightened his hold on his bicycle handles. "I don't care. You can keep your invitations a big secret."

"They're amazing!" Kavita shouted.

"Whatever," Jay hopped back on his bicycle and pedaled away. Jeff followed him.

"What about the Crumps?" Kavita asked me after a moment.

"I told you before. It'd be silly to invite them."

"I'll ask Jay what he thinks," Kavita said. Before I could say, no, she called, "Jay Davenport, come back here."

Jay stopped and looked back.

"Pleasie-please-please, Jay?" Kavita said in her sweet, singsong voice.

Jay leaned his bicycle against a tree and came bounding over like a kangaroo. "What?" he asked.

Why was he looking at me? "I didn't call you."

Kavita grabbed Jay's arm. "We have made a haunted tunnel and Nina isn't inviting the Crumps. Isn't that wrong?"

"Kavita, you just gave away our secret," I said.

She stomped her foot. "I did not."

"A haunted tunnel? Sounds cool. Where is it? Can I see it?" Jay asked.

I shook my head. "It's not done. And even if it were, I don't know if I want you to see it."

Jeff waved from down the street. "I'm leaving!"

Jay held up his hand to Jeff. "Wait, I'm coming." Then he looked at me and added, "I don't care about seeing your Halloween tunnel anyway."

"I'm sure plenty of kids will want to see it. So if you don't want to come, it's just fine by me," I said.

He walked away. This time he didn't bound away like a kangaroo.

"Jay, what about the Crumps?" Kavita shouted. "We should invite them, right?"

"Yes, go ahead and invite them. Invite the whole town."

Kavita turned to me. "See, I was right." Then she rode up the Crumps' driveway.

Jay had ruined everything.

After Kavita rang the Crumps' doorbell, I handed her an invitation. "Don't say anything. Just hand them this."

I was sure once Mr. and Mrs. Crump read that the haunted tunnel was for those twelve and under, they wouldn't want to come.

Mr. Crump opened the door. "Hey, Kavita, Nina."

I liked how perfectly he said our names. Unlike some other neighbors, Mr. Crump doesn't call us "girls" or "sweeties" or "kids." Mr. Crump always remembers that my sister is Kavita and I am Nina. Maybe it's because he sees us almost every single day.

"Here is an invitation for our haunted tunnel," Kavita said.

"It is for kids in the neighborhood, but we thought you might like an invitation," I explained.

"Is Mrs. Crump here?" Kavita asked.

I pulled her hand. "Let's not disturb her. We have lots of invitations to give out."

"I want to talk to her. Please," Kavita said. She slipped her hand from mine and peeked into the house. "Mrs. Crump?" she called.

Mrs. Crump came to the door.

Kavita turned to me. "See Nina, I was right. Mrs. Crump is small and skinny enough to fit in our tunnel. She won't get stuck."

I felt my face turning as red as Kavita's scooter. Mrs. Crump looked as confused as Mr. Crump. They kind of look alike when they are confused.

"Never mind. It's nothing important," I said to Mrs. Crump. I tried to drag Kavita away. "Come on, Kavita."

But she was stuck on the Crumps' steps and didn't budge. "You are the only grown-up who can go through the tunnel, Mrs. Crump. Will you come, please?" Kavita asked.

"I will come," Mrs. Crump said.

Oh no! Now I was embarrassed and wished I was far away. This was my fault. I should have never followed Kavita up the Crumps' driveway to their front door.

I was in serious trouble.

* I had already messed up the tunnel invite.

* Jay, who I wanted to come, wasn't coming.

* Mrs. Crump, who I didn't want to come, was coming.

* My haunted tunnel wasn't even finished.

It was time to go home.

"Let's finish the tunnel before we hand out the rest of the invitations," I said to Kavita. "Otherwise, we won't have anything to show anyone when they come."

"If we finish the tunnel and it gets dark, Mom won't let us go out to invite people to come see it. And if no one comes to see the tunnel, it will be sad."

I wanted to say, "Thanks to you, Mrs. Crump will." Instead I said, "You're right."

The rest of the invitation-giving went well. We went to Jay's house. Of course, he wasn't home. He was out with his new best friend, Jeff.

I gave Meera Masi the invitation. "Could you please give this to Jay?" I said.

She looked at it and said, "Your latest brainchild sounds exciting, Nina."

I didn't know your brain could have children. I wondered how many children my brain has? Maybe it even has some grandchildren. Do I know them? Does my brain know them? I wasn't sure. So I stayed quiet and just smiled.

I wondered if Meera Masi would remember to give the invitation to Jay. He was her one and only real child.

Now my brain was confused. It didn't know that I didn't know if I wanted him to come or not.

I was sure of one thing. I had to finish the tunnel. And I had to make it haunted. And I had to figure out my Halloween Queen costume, and it had to be as good as whatever Jay had planned.

Then I realized another thing. I had become so busy with the tunnel that I had not asked Mom about getting me a costume.

How could I go trick or treating without a costume?

No costume, no trick or treat, no candy.

"Do you know if Dad bought candy for Halloween yet?" I asked Kavita as we headed home.

"Dad and I did that a long time ago when we went grocery shopping. We bought two kinds of candy. Dad said he was going to get one more kind."

Great. At least we had some candy in the house. Still, I would be so sad if I couldn't go trick or treating with Jay and Kavita.

Was Jay going with us?

Or Jeff?

CHAPTER SIX

Dad was bagging up the last of the leaves in our front yard. Kavita parked the scooter in the garage and ran over to him, probably to ask if he bought more candy.

I went looking for Mom. She was in the kitchen.

"Do you have anything I could use for a queen kind of costume?" I asked.

She pointed at the table, where a tiara sat. "Megan's dad dropped this off for you. I didn't know you wanted to be a queen." She smiled. "How about the new langha outfit that you wore for Diwali? It's sparkly and queenlike."

I didn't want to wear my langha outfit. Jay had already seen it. Plus, I wanted to be a Halloween Queen not a Diwali Queen. I didn't say that to Mom. "It's too cold for langha."

"We could go buy something." Mom glanced at the clock.

"I don't think there will be anything good left. Let's look in your closet please?" Mom has a lot of Indian things in her closet and some of them are really cool. Maybe I could find something special there.

"Sure."

Kavita and Dad came in the kitchen. "Do you want to see the candy we have?" Kavita asked me.

"Not right now. You and Dad take care of the candy. I'll be right back."

Mom and I went to her room. She opened the closet. She showed me a few tops, all glittery, but I didn't think they were right for a Halloween Queen. So she showed me some of her saris and scarves. I shook my head.

I could feel tears pricking my eyes and I reached for a tissue box on a shelf.

That's when I saw something folded on a bottom shelf. It looked heavy, like a blanket and not light like a sari.

"What it that black thing?" I asked.

"That's a robe I had when I was your age. It was part of a play costume."

I held it up. It was dark, dark blue, not black. It was velvety and soft. It had shiny gold embroidery in the front.

"It's beautiful," I said.

"It's old and it has holes in the back," Mom said.

I turned it around. It did have several holes. They were tiny though.

"Could I use it?" I asked.

"Only if it fits you," Mom said. "I don't want you to trip and fall."

I tried it on and it fit perfectly.

I couldn't believe my luck. I had a Halloween Queen's regal robe!

"Mom, thank you." I gave her a big hug.

Sometime it is great to get lucky.

I came downstairs. Kavita had three bowls filled with three different kind of candies and was counting them. I was tempted to do the same, but we had to finish our tunnel.

"Kavita, just like the outside air, now I'm filled with freshness. Let's start working on making our tunnel beautiful outside and scary inside.

"Dad, can we have a candy?" she asked.

"Only one," Dad replied.

"Ladybugs are so cute. Can we make my ladybug lisible?" Kavita asked as she opened the candy wrapper.

"I told you before. Not lisible. *Visible*. Remember, it means that everyone can see it." I took a bite out of my candy.

"I know what it means. Sometimes I just don't know how to say it right," Kavita said.

"Don't worry. *V* is a difficult sound. Even Mom and Dad can't say it. Right, Dad?"

"Yes," he agreed. "Wisible," he said to prove it.

"Does that mean I won't be able to say it?" Kavita asked.

I took the last bite of my candy. "You were born here so you will learn the *V* sound. Just like me. Now let's wash our hands and go down to the basement," I said.

While Kavita and I created a new part of our tunnel, a welcoming room in the front, she sang. *"Wisible, isible, lisible, they all sound the same to me. If wisible is a word, why can't isible, lisible be?"*

I am so used to Kavita's singing that sometimes it doesn't bother me. Luckily, this was one of those sometimes.

We used four tall chairs to make two movable walls. It was easy to do. We draped a sari between two chairs and then did the same with the second sari and the other two chairs.

We moved Kavita's ladybug box into the middle of the welcoming space. We plopped it on a folding chair and made sure that the ladybug side was in the front. Then we blocked the two plain sides of the box with dupattas tied up with black ribbons.

Underneath the box, we hung a sign we'd made, that said *Dangerous Dark Tunnel Ahead*. We dimmed the wall lamp, so there was some light, but not too much. That way everyone would have to go through the room and meet Kavita's awesome ladybug.

Now the boxes were all set up and the ladybug room was there, but there was nothing scary about the tunnel, even though it was supposed to be haunted. Sure, there were pictures of bats and spiders, but we also needed some gooey, yucky, scary things.

Dad called us to help with dinner. We were having pizza tonight and Kavita and I always helped. We ran upstairs and washed our hands.

As I rolled out the dough, I had an idea.

Then Kavita stuck olives on each of the fingers on her left hand. Now she had five black olive fingertips.

"Look!" she said.

That gave me another idea.

I needed to help finish making dinner, but I couldn't wait to write my ideas down in Sakhi before I forgot.

"Are you pretending to be a wiggly earthworm?" Kavita asked.

"I'm not wiggling."

"Yes, you are."

I rolled my eyes but didn't answer her.

As soon as I was finished rolling out the dough, I washed my hands. Usually I waited for Kavita to brush the dough with olive oil and then I would spread the sauce and sprinkle toppings and cheese before Dad shoved the pizza into the oven. Today, I tried to leave the kitchen.

"Don't you want to help me sprinkle the toppings?" Kavita asked.

"No, thanks." Her face fell, so I quickly said, "You are big now. You can do it all by yourself."

She beamed.

I escaped to my room and wrote

Haunted tunnel needs

* Dough balls or something like that for stickiness

* Black olives for eyeballs (Then I thought of Jay's green eyes. So I added one more item below.)

* Green olives or grapes for green eyeballs

* Cardboard, cotton balls, and sheets to make mini ghosts

* String to hang the mini ghosts

* Fake blood (I didn't have money to buy fake blood. Maybe red pepper mixed with water would work.)

* Overcooked spaghetti to hang from the cardboard celling. Make it slimy by throwing a few okra pods into the pot while it cooked.
* Sticks and tissue papers, to make some more ghosts for gifts

It was easy to gather all the things on my list except for the fake blood. I went into the kitchen. The pizza was in the oven and the melting cheese smell made me hungry.

I needed to focus and figure out something to use for the fake blood. What did we have that was red?

I opened the spice box and took out the ground red pepper. Could I mix it with water? As soon as I took a spoonful, I sneezed and my eyes started to burn. I sneezed three times and my eyes began to water, I guess because red peppers are hot. I knew if everyone started sneezing and crying, they wouldn't have fun going through the tunnel. I placed the container of red pepper back into the spice box.

Next, I found the bottle of ketchup in the refrigerator. I squeezed some in a bowl. It was thicker than blood, so I added some water and stirred.

Kavita walked in. She sniffed and pointed at the bowl. "What are you eating with that runny ketchup?"

"Nothing," I said.

I guess ketchup was not the best choice for blood because everyone knew what it smelled like. I had to use something red that no one knew the smell of.

As I was putting the ketchup back in the refrigerator, I saw a bottle of pomegranate juice. That was something that most kids wouldn't recognize the smell of.

I poured some juice in another bowl. It was too thin. Blood couldn't be thin. Even thin people's blood is not thin. I know, because Dad is very thin, but his blood is not. Once when he pricked himself while cutting cabbage, he bled. His blood was just as thick as blood should be.

No one would be fooled by blood that looks like colored water.

It is easy to make thick things thin. Just add water. But how do you make thin pomegranate juice thick?

"Why are you looking like you have a problem?" Kavita asked.

"Because I do," I said. I wanted to say, "You're my problem, because you don't let me think in peace." But that would be mean, and I am not a mean sister. "We have to make this pomegranate juice thick, but I don't know how. I guess we could boil it down and let all the water evaporate."

"What does that mean?"

"Evaporate means you heat it up until the watery part becomes steam, and the remaining liquid gets thick."

"Then let's do that."

I poured some juice in a glass. "We will need a lot of it."

I took a sip. It tasted sour and sweet, like a pomegranate kind of herbal tea (which is just water with some mint or peppermint thrown in). I remembered when Mom let the water for tea boil and boil. Then it just started to disappear without getting thick. I wondered if the same thing would happen to the pomegranate juice. I took another sip.

"You are drinking it all up. There won't be any left to make fake blood," Kavita said.

I took a third sip and smacked my lips. "I don't think it would work."

"Then can I have some too?" Kavita asked.

She sure loves pomegranate, whether it's solid or liquid.

Dad came in and took the pizza out of the oven. Now it was time to eat. I stayed quiet about fake blood during dinner, but I kept thinking about what I could use to make some. When I took a bite of pizza, a string of cheese trailed from my mouth to the pizza. Along with the dough balls, the cheese was perfectly gooey, stringy, and sticky.

I noticed that Kavita's lips were red, because she had extra tomato sauce.

That's it. I could use tomato paste and add pomegranate juice to it to make it like blood. That way the blood wouldn't smell like tomato paste or pomegranate. It would be a mixture of the two and would have a very special smell that no one would know.

Now I had thought of everything!

I couldn't wait to get going on decorating the haunted tunnel using my new ideas.

Our invitation said for visitors to come from 1:00 to 3:30 p.m., so I would have to wake up early the next morning and get working on my plans.

Kavita and I stayed up and made ghost on sticks. Dad helped roll wads of tissue for ghost heads. I attached one to the end of a stick and then wrapped tissue paper around it, like a cape. Kavita drew eyes and mouth with a black marker. We made thirty of them and put them in an old shoebox. One less thing to do tomorrow!

I was happy I had figured out everything. But I was a little sad too. Even though I had invited Jay, he was mad and he probably wouldn't show up. I had thought I didn't care what he did, but I did care.

Maybe that's why that night my sleep came like it was a rabbit, all jumpy and jittery.

Or maybe it was because the next day was the haunted tunnel time. Queen-becoming day.

CHAPTER SEVEN

It was Halloween morning and I had still so much left to do.

I made a list and looked it over. It was a lot, but I thought I could get it all done in two hours. The only problem was, I kept getting new ideas. They were ideas that would make my haunted tunnel an even bigger success.

The problems with my ideas

* They don't take much time to arrive in my brain.

* But most of them require permission from Mom and Dad.

* Most of them take time to complete.

* And some of them just don't work out.

Still, I had to follow one of my new ideas, because it was too good to ignore.

Ig-nore means to pay no attention. I think "nore" sounds like "snore" and if you snore, you are asleep and you can't pay attention.

Anyway, I couldn't snore—I mean ignore—this idea. I gulped down my milk-soaked Cheerios in record time and changed into my clothes.

"Mom, can I come to the store with you this morning?" I asked.

Mom smiled. "That would be nice."

"Can I get some apple cider?" I asked while Mom was still smiling.

"Sure."

"For all the haunted tunnel visitors." I added, "I have money to pay for it."

"You do?"

"Well, kind of. I will get lots of money from the admission charge and I'll be able to pay you back later today."

"I'll give you five dollars. You pay the rest," Mom said.

Wow! The cider wouldn't cost more than ten dollars. That meant I would be getting at least half free. That's 50 percent off. Fifty percent off is a good bargain. Good luck was with me.

"Stay with me all day," I whispered to my good luck.

✳✳✳

Going to the store took a lot more time than I had expected. That's because we bought turnips, butternut squash, apples, honey, carrots, and Brussels sprouts. And, of course, apple cider. Then I saw an amazing sight: a table full of small, strange-looking squashes.

"I have never had a bumpy squash. Have you?" I asked Mom.

"They're usually not as good as the regular kind."

"Could we still buy a couple of them for the haunted tunnel?"

Mom laughed. "Now I know why you were interested in them. Pick out two."

We lugged all of our groceries to the car. Mom placed all the things she was carrying into the trunk and so did I.

I shut the trunk and turned around. "Fall is heavy, spring is light."

Mom opened the car door. "What do you mean?"

I put my seat belt on. "In spring we buy radishes, asparagus, peas, and strawberries and they don't weigh much. Today we bought all the heavy stuff."

"You are right, Nina. You get some excellent ideas and thoughts in that brain of yours!"

"Thanks." What Mom said made me so happy that I could have carried twice the weight of the groceries.

✳✳✳

By the time we got home, it was almost ten thirty. Kavita was waiting for me and we began working again on our tunnel right away.

I glued black olives on the warty squash heads and made them look even scarier. Mom helped us peel green and red grapes. Kavita and I stuck them inside of one of the smaller boxes.

When I told Mom that I was going to mix ketchup and pomegranate juice to make fake blood, she said, "But it will stain clothes."

Now I was stuck. I didn't want the haunted tunnel visitors to have stained clothes. I opened the refrigerator and looked at all the drinks. There were three different types of juices, milk, coconut water, and buttermilk. I stopped.

"Mom, buttermilk is thick and has a sour smell. What if I added red tempura paint to it? It doesn't stain. Would that be better?"

"Yes," she said. "It's also safe."

Perfect!

I poured the buttermilk into a bowl, added some red powder, and mixed. The fake blood was ready!

Next, I cut a hole in one of the boxes. Then I inflated a latex glove, pulled it over one end of an empty paper towel roll, and inserted it in the hole. I dipped the gloved hand in the fake blood and placed the bowl under it.

"Check out the blood-dripping hand. Doesn't it look scary?" I asked Kavita.

She glanced at it and shook her head. "Nope. It looks like a paper towel roll stuck in a glove. Looks all wrong."

Kavita was right. How could I make the paper towel roll look more like an arm?

I slipped a whole bunch of tiny bangles on the roll. We got them from India when I was little and now they didn't even fit Kavita.

"It's brown and full of bangles, just like our arms and hands. Great," Kavita said.

"Thanks."

Mom boiled some spaghetti with a couple of okra pods for a long time; it was the best-sticking overcooked spaghetti ever. We didn't even need glue to hang the strands on the squash heads.

"I like all the haunted stuff, but the wart heads are my favorite," Kavita said.

Wart heads. Kavita had the right word for the squashes.

Finally, I applied some mashed rice to the ceiling of the tunnel and stuck popcorn on it, to make it bumpy and warty too.

Then we put the boxes in a row to make the tunnel. It was time to crawl through it!

I turned off the lights and Kavita and I entered the tunnel.

"I can't see a thing," Kavita said.

She was right. I couldn't see a thing either. No blood, no bumpy tunnel, no scary faces, no bloody hand. Only darkness. I realized we had more than a speck of a problem, more than smudge of a problem, more than a spot of a problem. We had a show-stopping, tunnel-collapsing, mountain of a problem.

If Jay came now, and saw us in complete darkness without any of our hard work, he would laugh his head off.

I closed my eyes, even though it was dark and I didn't need to do that.

Another idea popped up in my brain. "We need flashlights," I said.

"I have one in my emergency kit," Kavita said.

Kavita had made an emergency kit two years ago when she learned about it in preschool. She keeps it under her bed and even changes the water bottle every month. Talk about being prepared.

"Great. Can you get it?"

"No. What if there is an emergency and we need

the flashlight while someone is using it for the haunted tunnel?"

"We won't have any emergency," I said.

Kavita put one hand on her hips and wagged the index finger of her other hand. "Remember, an emergency comes without knocking. That's why we have to be prepared for it." She sounded like her teacher Mrs. Jabs.

I had another brilliant idea. "Kavita, this *is* an emergency. We have the most amazing haunted tunnel, but no one can see it. We need a flashlight. Only you can help."

She threw up her hands. "I guess this *is* an emergency." Then she left.

A few minutes later, Kavita returned with two flashlights.

"How did you get two of them?"

"Dad has his own emergency kit."

"That's perfect."

"I know." She twirled. "And I'm perfectly awesomer. Nina, we better not have any other emergencies now, OK?"

"No way," I said.

My perfectly awesomer sister and I crawled through the haunted tunnel with our flashlights. Our tunnel was scary and spooky. I couldn't wait for kids to try it out.

I couldn't wait for Jay to go through.

The only problem was, I didn't know if he was going to show up at all.

CHAPTER EiGHT

Dad had made turnip, carrot, and ginger soup for lunch but Kavita and I were too excited to eat.

"I'm not hungry," I told him.

He said. "OK, you can eat your soup later."

That was a good idea. My stomach had turned into a jumpy popcorn popper and I needed to calm down. I had to look regal in my gold-embroidered robe.

"We only have one hour before everyone arrives. Let's change. Go get your costume on," I said to Kavita.

"What costume?" she asked.

"The butterfly outfit Meera Masi made you for Halloween."

"I can't wear that now. I might ruin it," she said. "The wings won't fit in the tunnel."

Then I realized I couldn't wear my Halloween Queen costume either. My costume was just too beautiful to wear for the haunted tunnel. I might also ruin it. Plus, no royal would ever crawl on her hands and knees. Nor could I run up and down the stairs in it. If I tripped and sprained my ankle, I wouldn't be able to go trick or treating.

I needed a different costume for Nina Soni, Haunted-Tunnel-Halloween-Queen. It had to be practical.

Prac-ti-cal means something that is going to work the best.

Kavita and I had used all our time creating the haunted tunnel. Now I had nothing special to wear. I went to my closet and stood there, staring at my clothes. If I could create the haunted tunnel, I could create my haunted costume.

I slipped on a black leotard, a T-shirt, and a pair of black pants. Then I spotted an orange hard hat. Uncle Ryan, Jay's dad, had given it to me. He's in the construction business. Black and orange were Halloween colors so my outfit was appropriate for the holiday, but kind of plain.

I quickly decorated my clothes and hat with more pictures of spiders and bats. Now I would match the tunnel

Kavita came in and watched me for a few seconds. Then she asked, "Can I put some dots on your hat?"

"Sure."

When she was done, I put on the hat and looked in the mirror. I didn't look scary at all. "I should have made a mask," I told Mom when she came to check on us.

"You look spidery to me," Mom said.

"No, I just look like Nina with long black arms and legs."

"Like a daddy longlegs," Mom suggested.

"It would be scary if I really looked like one." I made a mean face.

I really don't know what a daddy longlegs' face looks like, because I haven't looked at one that carefully. But I imagined it would be mean. And my mean face was definitely scarier than my regular face.

"Where is Kavita?" I asked. I hadn't even realized she was gone.

"In her room," Mom said. "I think you inspired her."

I poked my head into Kavita's room. "What're you doing?"

"Can you write APHID on this shirt?" Kavita asked, handing me an old green shirt and a marker. "In big letters?"

I wondered why Kavita wanted me to write the name of tiny white insects that suck juice of plants. But I didn't ask.

I sat down in the hallway and wrote APHID. Then she took her shirt and disappeared into her room again. She even closed her door.

I waited and waited.

Finally, I knocked. "Come on out."

When Kavita came out, I saw that her green shirt and brown pants were covered with drawings of dark green aphids. Not real ones, thank goodness.

"Why have you drawn aphids on your clothes?" I asked her.

"I am a rose branch covered in aphids, silly. To go with the dots on your hat that are ladybugs."

"My hat doesn't have ladybugs," I said. "They're just dots. Plus, there are spiders and bats as well."

"The dots are ladybugs. Remember, I drew them, so I know what they are. You have to use your imagination."

"You really want ladybugs to be part of Halloween," I said.

"Yes. Now they are."

"What do you mean?"

"Well, what was the very first Halloween like?" Kavita asked.

I shrugged. "I don't know. I wasn't there."

"But someone must have been there. People must have started it, right?"

"I guess so," I said.

"They must have thought about what the things were. And they came up with ghosts and bats and other scary things, right?" Kavita asked.

"Yes, but those *are* all scary things. Ladybugs are not. They are kind of cute."

"Ladybugs eat aphids so they are scary for aphids," she said. "I am a rose branch with aphids." She pointed to herself. "My aphids are all scared of your ladybugs."

I rolled my eyes. I didn't even try to tell her that I was supposed to be the Haunted Tunnel Halloween Queen.

"Nina, Kavita, come downstairs," Dad called.

"Is Dad waiting for our haunted tunnel?" Kavita asked. "He is skinny, but I don't think he can fit inside."

"Maybe he wants some apple cider."

When we went down, Dad was pacing with his arms behind him. He didn't look like someone thirsty for apple cider. He looked seriously glum. I wondered what we had done wrong.

I knew the best thing would be to ask him if he was OK before he said anything to us. I even asked him in Hindi. "Sub kuchh theek hai, Dad?"

"Haan, I mean na. My flashlight is missing from my emergency kit."

I made a quick in-my-head-list.

* Dad said, haan, which means yes.

* Then he said, na, which means no.

* He was confused for sure.

* This really was an emergency.

* Is that why he was checking his emergency kit? (It was sitting on the table. I wondered where he usually kept it.)

"Nina has it," Kavita answered, faster than you could flick on a flashlight. Maybe not. Maybe the in-my-head list making took longer than I thought.

Dad turned to me. "Shouldn't you have asked me first?"

"I didn't take it," I said. "I don't even know where you keep your emergency kit."

"I keep it in that cupboard and check it at the end of each month to make sure everything is in order."

Kavita jumped in. "Dad, you replace the water and snacks. Right?"

"You are very observant, Kavita." Dad smiled at her. "I also make sure the flashlight batteries work." Then Dad said, "You must have taken the flashlight and now you are blaming your sister. That's not a right thing to do, Kavita."

I glance at the clock. It was 12:26. We only had thirty-four minutes before our visitors arrived! If Dad started telling Kavita what was the right thing to do it might take a long time. "Don't worry, Dad. Kavita and I are working together. And the batteries work just fine too."

"That's not the point. You should have asked me before you took the flashlight. What if there was an emergency and we needed it?"

"We did have an emergency." Kavita pointed at me. "Nina said so."

We're having one right now, I wanted to say. Instead I said, "Sorry about that, Dad. May we use your flashlight?"

"Sure, as long as you return it to me."

"We will. Do you want to see our tunnel real quick?" I asked.

Dad and Mom both came downstairs. But they couldn't go through the tunnel. "I like what you have done with saris and scarves," Mom said.

"Make sure everyone has their permission slip before you let them through the tunnel," Dad said.

"And their admission fee," I said.

Mom and Dad laughed.

The last thing Kavita and I did was to set up paper cups, napkins, and a pitcher of apple cider on the kitchen counter. Mom poured the cups and put them in a tray.

It was twelve forty now. We had twenty minutes before our haunted tunnel was open for business.

"Let's go outside and grab the first kid who walks by our house," I suggested. "We can ask her to go through the tunnel. She can have a free run—I mean free crawl—and we'll get to know how she likes it."

"You can pretend she is an aphid and you are a ladybug," Kavita said. "But she could be a he too."

How easily Kavita had turned me from the queen to ladybug! "Sure."

But no one was outside, or even on their way to our house. Kavita and I sat on our front steps and waited.

Shouldn't kids be lining up by now? For most of them this was going to be their first haunted tunnel. Why wasn't there more excitement? We should have planned ahead and spread the word.

Kavita stood up. "This waiting is making me hungry. I am going in." Before I could answer her, she shouted, "Jay! There is Jay!"

He sauntered over. He was wearing regular clothes. If he had a special costume, wouldn't he wear it? I wondered if he was coming over to see the tunnel or just checking to see if anyone was coming to our haunted tunnel.

"Get up, ladybug," Kavita said to me.

"Ladybug Nina?" Jay looked at my costume.

Kavita tugged at his hand. "Come, aphid, come."

Jay frowned. "What are aphids?"

"Aphids are tiny white insects," I said.

"I'm a rose branch covered with aphids." Kavita twirled. "See?"

"I am certainly not an aphid," Jay said.

"Not for real," I said quickly. I didn't want him to leave.

"Just like you aren't the Halloween Queen!" he said.

Kavita grabbed his hand again and pulled him to our front steps. "Come on, check out our haunted tunnel. It is awesome. You won't even get scared. Right, Nina?"

"He's supposed to get scared," I said.

"Ha! You think I'll get scared by your puny little haunted tunnel?" Jay said. "Not a chance."

Who was Jay to call our haunted tunnel puny? "Why don't you come and see for yourself, Mr. Not-Scared?"

"I will." He dug in his pocket and pulled out a crumpled bill. "One dollar, right?"

At least Jay had money, he wasn't with Jeff, and I didn't have to beg him to visit our haunted tunnel.

Even without the robe, it certainly made me feel like the Halloween Queen.

CHAPTER NiNE

Meera Masi must have given Jay the invitation and he must have read it carefully. That's why he had the exact amount of money in his pocket.

Maybe he'd been planning to come. That possibility made me feel like a shiny bright ladybug on a lovely June day. I kept quiet about a free crawl. I mean, he already had the money so why not take it?

"That's right. One dollar." I held out my palm.

He didn't deposit the money into it. "What if I don't like your tunnel? Do I get my money back?"

"Sure," Kavita said before I could answer.

"No. This is not the kind of thing where you get your money back if you don't like it. Disney World doesn't let you do that."

He grinned. "Oh, so you think you are like Disney?"

Mr. Grinface, you think you're too smart, I thought. I didn't say it out loud, because I needed my first person to crawl through the tunnel. "Give me the money," I mumbled.

"What did you say?" he asked.

"Nothing. Here is the deal. If you truly don't like our tunnel you can get your money back, but if you like it, you can help us get the neighborhood kids to come. You can help promote our Halloween Tunnel."

To **pro-mote** means to go out and tell people how great something is, so everyone wants to come.

"That sounds like a good deal." Jay deposited the dollar in my palm. My fingers curled around it.

"It's a great deal," Kavita said. "Because you are our very first haunted tunnel visitor. And it's—"

"Amazing," I said.

We went in the house. He saw apple cider on the counter. "Yum!"

"Later." I handed one of the flashlights to Jay. I carried the other one.

"I need a flashlight?" he asked.

"Duh, how else will you see the scary stuff?" I said.

"OK," he said.

"Follow me." I turned on my flashlight as Kavita and Jay followed me down the steps. My heart pounded. Would Jay like our tunnel or think it was puny?

"Ta da!" Kavita said as we stepped into the welcoming room. She pointed to the tunnel door.

Jay went through the refrigerator box door. Then he came right back out. "I can't walk through the next part. It's not tall enough, Nina."

"This is a haunted tunnel not a haunted palace," I told

him. "You have to get on your hands and knees and crawl through."

Kavita burst out singing, *"Just pretend you're an earthworm or an aphid. Drop, crawl, and creep along."*

"Only if you stop singing, Kavita," he said.

Kavita zipped her mouth. Jay went in again. I heard the sounds of him wiggling. I grabbed the other end of the bangled hand and waited. As he passed through that box, I lowered it into the bowl of fake blood. I thought he would say "gross" or "ouch," but he was silent.

I dipped it again.

"Stop it," he said.

I tried not to laugh.

"Do you see my grape eyeballs? The green ones are your eyes," Kavita shouted. "Aren't they amazing?"

"They are. Much better than the dripping bangle roll," Jay shouted back.

"Wait until—" Kavita started to say, but I covered her mouth before she spilled the next thing he'd encounter.

En-coun-ter means when you come across something. And it might be nice, or difficult or even scary.

I held my breath. When I saw a faint light coming out
of the box with the warty squashes, I shrieked at the top
of my lungs.

Silence.

When Jay came out of the tunnel. I turned the overhead
light on.

"Well?" I asked.

"This is good," he said.

"Good? It is *awesome*," Kavita said. "You weren't scared, right?"

Jay glanced at me. "I...I don't think I was."

I picked up a stick ghost and twirled it. "Speak the truth."

"I guess just a little. By those weird warty things and your screaming."

I handed him his very own ghost for telling the truth.

"Say, I have an idea," he said. "I am going to dress up as King Yama for Halloween. Maybe I can help you with the tunnel."

"You what?" I almost flopped down on one of my tunnel boxes. Yama was the King of Death in the Indian stories that Meera Masi shared with us. It was wonderful that Jay thought to dress up like Yama. I was excited and a little jealous of him.

"It's only five minutes before the tunnel opening time.

Let's go up. If I'm going to change into my costume, I have to do it now," Jay said.

"He has Yama's crown and everything," Kavita said as she climbed up the stairs.

"You knew about it? How come you never told me, Kavita?" I asked following her.

"Because it was a secret and I am good at keeping a secret."

"Then how come you can't keep some of my secrets?" I asked, I remembered how she almost told Jay that the first tunnel visitor could go for free.

"Kavita kept your secret. She didn't tell me anything about this haunted house," Jay said as we reached the top.

I looked out the window. Still not a single kid was out there.

"Haunted *tunnel*," Kavita corrected. "Remember, you had to crawl through it."

"How could I forget?" He moved his head in a circle. "I'm still trying to get the kink out of my neck."

"Did your mom tell you to dress up as Yama?" I asked Jay.

"Nope, it was my very own idea. I thought everyone dresses up as ghosts and witches so why can't I be Yama? I have Indian clothes and my mom made me a gold crown."

"His crown is awesome," Kavita said.

Yama would be great to have as a welcoming person, but the haunted tunnel was my idea. Kavita and I had done all of the work. Jay didn't want money for helping us. But I didn't want Jeff to show up, if Jay was here. Jay hadn't mentioned him, so maybe Jeff had gone home.

With or without Jeff, did I want to share the haunted tunnel with Jay?

I made in-my-head list.

* Jay was my best friend.

* I had wanted him to work on the tunnel.

* That hadn't worked out, but now he was offering to help.

| ✳ | It would be fun to have him be part of it now. |
| ✳ | Maybe with his help we would have more visitors. |

"You can help," I said.

"I also have a fake skeleton to make sure everyone understands that Yama is in the death business," Jay said. "Hey, what if I wait on the front steps? I will be the welcoming person for the haunted tunnel."

I thought about it for a second. "I think even the fake skeleton would scare little kids like James and Eric. Plus, I have never seen Yama with a skeleton."

"What if I don't bring it?"

"That would work." There was still nobody waiting to visit the haunted tunnel. "I can't pay you, Jay. We have to pay my mom for the cider."

"No worries. I'll take some free cider," Jay said.

"At our house you always get everything for free," I said.

Jay pointed at the paper cups. "Now these are puny little cups. I want more than that."

He took a glass from the cupboard and filled it with cider, and gulped it down. He wiped his mouth with the back of his hand.

It was already past the opening time. *What if no one else comes?* I thought.

As if he could read my mind, Jay said, "Don't worry. Kids will come. I'd better go get dressed."

Now that King Yama—I mean Jay—was going to promote us, maybe we would get more visitors. Anyway, because of Jay, it was already much more fun!

CHAPTER TEN

Three of Kavita's friends, Avery, James, and Eric, arrived before Jay came back.

"I want some cider now," James said as soon as he stepped in the house.

Kavita pointed to the basement door. "You have to go through the haunted tunnel before you get your drink."

"Do they have permission slips and money?" I asked Kavita.

Kavita handed me permission slips and and three dollars she had already collected. "Yup. A dollar for the haunted tunnel, free apple cider, and a stick ghost."

"OK, that works," I said.

I gave Avery a flashlight. "Do I get to keep it?" she asked.

"No, you don't," I said. "You only use it when you go through the tunnel."

"I'm scared to go through the tunnel," she said. "I just want free apple cider."

"You have to go through the tunnel if you want free apple cider," Kavita said. "That's the rule."

"You have a flashlight, so it won't be dark," I said, as we went down the stairs.

Since these were all young, I decided not to make the haunted tunnel scarier by screaming.

Avery took the flashlight from my hand. I turned off the basement lights. She entered the tunnel, and Kavita and I waited and waited and waited for her to come out.

Finally, I called, "Avery? Avery?"

"Maybe she's taking a nap," Kavita said.

"No, I am not taking a nap," Avery said. "I'm making a picture with this red puddle of paint."

"That's not paint. That's blood," I said.

"Yuck!" Avery yelled and came crawling out as fast as she could.

"What's that sour, stinky smell?" James asked.

Avery waved her blood-soaked fingers in James's face. "Blood."

James looked like he was about to faint.

Kavita said, "It's just buttermilk with red tempura paint."

"You can't give away our secrets," I told her.

"If you do, Yama will grab you," a spooky, gravelly voice said.

Everyone turned around in the direction of the voice. Jay stood there, wearing a hideous mask and a shiny crown. He was scary and not scary at the same time.

"Who are you?" James asked.

"I am Yama, the King of Death," Jay said.

"Who are you, really?" James asked.

"No more questions," I said.

"You better hurry, James. Soon we'll have other kids wanting to visit the haunted tunnel," Yama said.

James entered the tunnel.

"Goodbye forever!" Yama said.

Before Jay could say more I whispered, "Don't scare him."

"I will follow your order, mighty ladybug queen." Yama bowed. His crown came tumbling down.

I laughed.

He picked up his crown and hurried back upstairs.

When James and Eric were done, I handed stick ghosts to them and Avery. Eric put his right back into the shoebox.

"Time for some apple cider," I said.

Since there were no more visitors, I followed them upstairs.

Max and Stella showed up soon after they left.

Jay said, "Welcome to my kingdom of death."

His kingdom of death? How dare Jay take credit for

all the tunnel work that Kavita and I had done! I glared at him.

"I am making it more fun," he whispered.

"It's not *your* kingdom," I said.

Jay shrugged. "Just playing my role as King of Death."

Maybe Jay felt powerful. When you are King Yama no one can hurt you. Anyway, I didn't have time to argue with him because Kavita was already leading Max and Stella into the house.

Jay collected their permission slips and Kavita gave each of them a flashlight and pointed to the steps to the basement. I rushed down, just ahead of them.

I made Max and Stella wait at the bottom of the steps while I took their money. I let Max enter the welcoming room and made Stella wait outside. If he saw what I was doing with the hand or screaming, he would be expecting it when his turn came. After Max came out, I let Stella go in. When she was done, I gave each of them a stick ghost and led them upstairs.

In the kitchen, Kavita took the flashlights and offered them cider.

As soon as they left, three more kids came down. Then two more. Finally, we had a break. That's when Kavita and I ran outside and waited with Jay for our next visitors. We didn't wait long.

Mario and Ramon, eight-year-old twins, showed up next. Jay introduced himself in a gravelly voice, saying, "I am Yama, King of Death. You two came into this world together. Do you expect to go through my kingdom together?"

Mario and Ramon looked confused or scared. I couldn't tell.

"Do you?" King Yama repeated.

"I think so," Mario said.

"You don't know for sure? This is a serious matter. Think about it." King Yama scowled.

Jay was trying to impress Mario and Ramon, but what if he frightened them away?

I said, "You can both go down to the basement at the same time but you must take turns going through the haunted tunnel."

They nodded.

Jay took their permission slip and said, "Enjoy the land of Yama."

I still didn't like that Jay had renamed *our* haunted tunnel as *his* land. The haunted tunnel that was my brainchild! I didn't like him taking credit for it. I couldn't stay quiet. "It's a haunted tunnel, not the land of Yama, and I am the Halloween Queen and its creator."

Mario and Ramon looked more confused.

"Come on in," Kavita said.

Jay and I were both quiet. Maybe it wasn't a good idea for me to greet visitors with him. Sometimes, it was best to let Jay do his own stuff as long as it didn't hurt anyone. Jay was directing everyone toward the basement and that was great for the haunted tunnel.

I took Mario and Ramon downstairs and they paid their admission. Mario went through the tunnel first. While

Ramon was crawling through it, Kavita came bounding down the stairs.

"Jeff is here," she whispered.

"Does he want to go through the haunted tunnel?" I asked while I lowered the bloody hand. I heard Ramon squeak in surprise.

"I don't know." Kavita looked confused. Most of the time, it's Kavita who confuses other people. She is usually so sure of herself.

"Why are you whispering?" I asked.

"Because Jeff is making fun of Yama. It's not nice to make fun of the King of Death, is it?"

"I hope they don't have a fight and ruin our fun," I said. "Poor Jay."

"Jay is not poor. He is powerful." Kavita turned around. "I need to go back upstairs. Mario is waiting for his cider."

"Yes, go," I said.

"Go where?" Jay asked as he came down the stairs. Jeff was right behind him. Why had they come down here?

"Nothing," I said.

Jeff turned the light on.

"You should go through the tunnel, Jeff. It's awesome," Kavita said.

Jeff rolled his eyes.

At the tunnel.

In front of us.

Sure, I roll my eyes sometimes but there is a reason for it. Jeff rolled his without bothering to crawl through the tunnel.

Jay looked away. I think he was embarrassed by his cousin's response.

I think King Yama—I mean Jay—was not happy.

Jeff folded his arms. "Jay, are you coming with me?"

Suddenly there was a shriek.

Jeff looked alarmed. "Who was that?"

"You could go through the tunnel and find out for yourself," I said.

Jeff tapped his foot. Like his foot was making the decision and not his brain.

Jay shrugged. "You said we'd meet at five-thirty and it's only three."

Ramon came out of the tunnel.

"Why did you scream?" Jeff asked him.

"When Mario went in, I heard someone scream. It didn't happen when I was in there, so I decided to do it myself."

"Sorry you didn't get a scream," I said.

"I'm leaving," Jeff said.

"Bye, Jeff," Kavita said.

Jay looked so sad that I wanted to tell him that it was OK for him to go too. But he also looked kind of mad.

Why was Jeff trying to take away Jay from all the fun?

Maybe Jeff was jealous of our friendship. Maybe he liked to be bossy.

I stayed quiet, because I didn't want to get between the cousins and get crushed.

Jay must want to stay. He had said so. I wished Jeff would go ahead and leave. I stared at the haunted tunnel, wondering what would happen.

"Bye, Jeff," Kavita said again.

CHAPTER ELEVEN

Mario emerged from the tunnel. "Estupendo!" He spread his arms wide.

"What does that mean?" Kavita asked.

When did he go through the tunnel again? I wondered

"Estupendo means great!" Mario said. He looked happy.

"It doesn't look great," Jeff muttered.

"Have you tried it?" Mario asked.

"I don't want to." Jeff's arms were still folded in front of him. He looked like he had taken a bite out of a bitter melon. "Well?" he said to Jay.

Then Ramon came out of the tunnel. He gave Mario, Jay, Kavita, and me each a high five. He tried to do the same with Jeff, but that high five fell down because Jeff didn't put up his palm. That didn't bother Ramon. He was still smiling, ear-to-ear.

I didn't ask Ramon why he also went through the tunnel twice.

Mario whispered to Ramon in Spanish.

"What are you two talking about?" I asked.

Mario handed me two more dollars. His eyes sparkled. "You should do this tunnel next year. We will come again." Then they both said, "Thank you."

"Have a cup of apple cider. It's in the kitchen," Kavita said. "Actually, you can have two cups because you paid twice, OK?"

"Muchas gracias!" They handed me their flashlights.

"You're welcome," I said. "Jay, shouldn't you wait outside?"

He wasn't listening to me.

"Well, Jay?" Jeff asked.

"Why do you keep saying 'well' over and over again? This is a haunted tunnel, not a well," Kavita said.

"I am not talking about a water well," Jeff said. "I'm saying 'well what—'"

"Jay doesn't know anyone named Well either. There is no Well or Will or Willy here. I am a rose branch with aphids, Nina wanted to be a Halloween Queen, but now she is spiders and ladybugs. And Jay is the King of Death, Yama." Kavita put her hands on her hips. "No Well here. Do you understand?"

Jeff was so stunned, he looked like he had swallowed a thorny rose branch.

We were having such a great time. Why did Jeff have to ruin it?

"I am leaving." Jeff turned away. I wondered how many times he had said that.

"I will see you at five thirty," Jay said. Now he looked sad.

"Would you like to go through the tunnel, Jeff?" I asked. Even though he had rolled his eyes, I still offered.

I did it more for Jay than Jeff. They were cousins and I didn't want Jeff to be mad at Jay because of the tunnel or because of Kavita and me.

"Even if I don't pay you?" Jeff asked.

"Yeah." I handed a flashlight to him. "It's OK."

Jay mouthed "Thanks."

It made me happy that Jay didn't look sad anymore.

Jeff went in the tunnel.

"I hear voices from upstairs. Sounds like more kids have arrived. I should greet them," Jay said.

Kavita and Jay went upstairs. I couldn't hear any noise coming out of the tunnel. I crossed my fingers, hoping Jeff was enjoying it. And even if he wasn't, I hoped he would stay quiet about it.

I listened closely and when Jeff was in the right place, I lowered the bloody hand and screamed. He screamed back.

When Jeff came out, his face was red, but he was smiling.

"That was great. Thanks." He handed me a dollar.

"Were you planning to come all along?" I asked.

"Shhh." He put his finger on his lips. "Don't tell Jay that I paid. It will drive him crazy that I got in for free."

"It will?"

"Yes. Don't you think?"

"I don't know," I replied.

Jeff had really confused me. What was he trying to do? Did he want to come between Jay and me? Or did he enjoy making troubles? I thought about what had happened.

* Jeff wanted Jay to leave early.

* He rolled his eyes and made fun of our tunnel.

* When I invited him to go through it, he said he couldn't pay me.

* But he had the money.

* Jeff thought it would drive Jay crazy that he got in for free.

| * | Jay had smiled and said thank you when I told Jeff he didn't have to pay. |
| * | I didn't think Jeff was right. Jay wasn't jealous or even upset about it. |

"I know Jay," Jeff said. "It will bug him that I didn't pay."

I had to stand up for Jay and for me. "No. Jay wouldn't care if you got in for free or not."

Jeff looked a little shocked. Was it because he found out Jay wouldn't care or because I disagreed with him?

One thing I was sure of. I knew Jay better than Jeff did.

Kavita came downstairs with Avery and James. I wondered if I should have made it clear that one dollar was per person, per admission.

Before I could tell them anything, Kavita said, "You can look at the ladybug, but you can't go through the tunnel again. Not without paying."

Avery's face fell, but James took money from his pocket.

He handed it to me. "Go on," I said to James. He picked up a flashlight.

"James, this time I get to go first. Wait for me, I'll be right back," Avery said and ran upstairs.

She was back in record time. Her face was glowing. "I can go again!" She handed me money.

How could she have gone home and returned with the money so quickly? "Where did you get the money?" I asked.

"I borrowed it from your mom."

"You can't do that," Kavita said. "Our mom has *our* money. You have to bring your own."

She looked confused. "I borrowed it," she said.

"And you'll pay it back, right?" I asked.

"I don't have to. I borrowed it," she insisted.

Kavita stomped her foot. "But that's not right! We need YOUR money."

Avery started crying. I didn't want Mom to come down and make a fuss about it. I said, "The second admission is half price so you and James both can go in from the money he paid."

"Then can we go in third time with the money I borrowed from your mom?"

Avery had me trapped. "You like good deals, right?" I asked her.

She nodded.

"The deal is: 50 percent off if the money is not borrowed. But you pay 100 percent of the price if any money is borrowed."

I crossed my fingers. I hope Avery didn't take the 50 percent off deal with James, then go a third time herself with the borrowed dollar from Mom. That would be 100 percent of the price.

She thought for a second. "I will take the 50 percent off."

Avery went in first. James waited for his turn. Kavita screamed. There was no response. I guess the second time through the tunnel was not scary. She didn't come out.

"Are you stuck?" Kavita shouted.

"No."

"Are you painting with fake blood, Avery?" I asked.

"No."

"Then what are you doing?" James asked.

"I am eating popcorns."

"You aren't allowed to eat the roof of the haunted tunnel!" Kavita shouted.

"Avery, come out. Now," I said in my Halloween Queen roar.

When Avery came out, her face was smeared with smooshed rice and pieces of popcorn.

James went in.

When I lowered the bangled hand and screamed, he didn't react.

I wondered what the tunnel roof looked like now but decided not to interrupt James to check. Maybe he could tell us. Good thing it was past three fifteen. The visiting hours for the haunted tunnel were almost over. If the roof was crumbling, it wouldn't fall on someone.

"Make sure you give our borrowed money back," Kavita said to Avery.

"I don't have to."

Here we go again, I thought. "Avery, when you borrow something you have to return it," I told her. "If you don't return it, then it is stealing. You don't want to be a thief, right?"

"Avery, you're my friend. Not a thief," Kavita said.

Avery handed me the money.

James came out with his palm covering his nose and mouth. He rushed upstairs. He must not like the smell of smooshed rice, I thought.

Avery followed him, and Kavita followed Avery.

I plopped down on the last stair. *Hieesh*!

Hieesh is like *phew*—saying it means you are happy to be done with your project. I was done with Avery and James. No more dealing with money or roof-eating problems.

I was happy and kind of sad that haunted tunnel time was almost over.

In-my-head list of what made me happy

* I was able to come up with a creative idea.

* It was fun to build the tunnel with Kavita.

* Jay had helped with the visitors.

* Our project was a success.

In-my-head list of what made me sad

* The tunnel time was over.

* Jay would leave soon.

* We had to clean up.

* I didn't know if Jay was going to trick or

treat with us.

CHAPTER TWELVE

After I rested for five minutes, I walked back upstairs. I was glad Avery and James weren't hanging around, borrowing more money from Mom and trying to enter the tunnel a third time.

Jay had come in the house. I pointed at the clock. "We're almost done."

"It was fun," he said, taking off his crown. "Why did James bolt out of here as if his pants were on fire?"

I shrugged. "Don't really know."

"Are you saying James is a liar?" Kavita asked.

"He's not a liar," I said.

Kavita stuck out her chin. "Jay said he ran like his pants were on fire! Like liar, liar, pants on fire!"

Jay shook his head. "That's just a saying."

"So why did you say the saying?" Kavita asked.

We were going in circles and I knew the only way out of it was to create a diversion.

Di-ver-sion means you leave whatever you are doing and dive for something else.

Kavita needed to dive for something else. I offered her some help by trying the change the subject. "It was a good turnout. I think most everyone we invited came through. Right, Kavita?"

She looked out the window. She had already forgotten about liar, liar, pants on fire. This was working.

"It was *perfect*," Jay said. "You should have invited everyone from school too."

"I didn't even think about that. I wished I had asked Megan and Tyler to come."

"Next year," Jay said.

"I wonder why Mrs. Crump hasn't come," Kavita said.

Mrs. Crump was not who I wanted Kavita to dive for. "She must be taking an afternoon nap," I said.

"I don't want her to miss the haunted tunnel. I'll go and remind her to come."

The only way to stop Kavita from going to the Crumps' house was to find something else for her to do. Another diversion.

"It is finally time to eat your soup," Dad said. Sometimes Dad creates a perfect diversion without even trying.

Jay, Kavita and I ate turnip, carrot, and ginger soup with sunflower seeds and croutons. Yummy!

✳✳✳

Just as we were finished with our soup, someone knocked on the front door. I went to open it.

"Mr. Crump," I said. My voice came out squeaky with surprise. I wanted Kavita to forget about Mrs. Crump, but how was it possible now? Plus, we were past the tunnel-crawling time. What were we going to do?

Kavita came running to the door. "Mr. Crump, Mr. Crump!" She held his hands and jumped up and down. "Where is Mrs. Crump? Doesn't she want to go through our haunted tunnel?"

The haunted tunnel was big enough for kids but I was afraid it was too small for adults. Even short and skinny adults like Mrs. Crump.

"She is waiting for a batch of cookies to cool down. She will be here soon." His eyes twinkled, like Santa's at Christmas. If Mr. Crump knew how Mrs. Crump would have to crawl to go through the tunnel he wouldn't have been so merry.

Then Mrs. Crump rolled in. I say rolled in because she was dressed as a plump, yellow-orange pumpkin! She is usually so skinny. She must have worked hard to look like a real pumpkin. She handed me a platter. Even though I was full, the scent of chocolate made my mouth water.

Kavita burst into: *"Mrs. Crump-kin, Mrs. Crump-kin, you're a beautiful pump-kin."*

And repeated it. *"Mrs. Crump-kin, Mrs. Crump-kin, you're a beautiful pump-kin."*

I cringed, looked away, and didn't know what to do.

But Mrs. Crump-kin—I mean Mrs. Crump—laughed.

"Do you want me to take you to the haunted tunnel?" Kavita asked.

"Yes, please do."

Was Mrs. Crump planning to go through the tunnel? My mouth flew open and Jay's did too.

Kavita took her downstairs. Mr. Crump, Jay, and I followed them.

"See our haunted tunnel?" Kavita said. "I think you're the only adult who can fit…"

Kavita didn't finish the sentence. She must have just realized that, dressed as a pumpkin, Mrs. Crump was too gol matol to go through the haunted tunnel.

> Gol matol is Hindi for something that is round and plump, like the letter O.

Mrs. Crump turned a complete circle to show us what she looked like from the sides and back. "Don't you think a roly-poly pumpkin would have a hard time going through the tunnel?"

"A pumpkin could get stuck," Kavita agreed. "Maybe next year you should dress up as a carrot, so you can go through the tunnel."

"It might be difficult for you to go down to the basement in a carrot costume," I added.

"I am sure I can manage," Mrs. Crump said.

Then Mr. and Mrs. Crump admired all the artwork we had done.

"I think this is the first time I have seen ladybugs for Halloween. This may be a start of something new," Mrs. Crump said.

Kavita beamed. "That's what I think too."

Mrs. Crump was a good neighbor because

✳ She came over to see our haunted tunnel.

✳ She made Kavita happy by admiring her work.

* She wore a pumpkin costume, which meant she didn't have to go through the tunnel.
* She even called Kavita's idea about dressing as a carrot wonderful.
* Mrs. Crump was wonderful.
* I was feeling wonderful with all the wonderful things happening.

OK, now I was tired of the word. No more wonderful again.

When we went up, Mom and Dad asked Mr. and Mrs. Crump to stay for tea. My parents were also wonderful, I mean good neighbors.

CHAPTER THIRTEEN

I glanced at the clock. It was already four thirty. "That was fun but now we have to clean up before trick or treating."

"First we have too much fun and now we have to do too much work," Kavita said.

"I can help," Jay said.

"What about Jeff?" I asked. "Don't you have to go?"

"Not for another hour."

Jay, Kavita, and I took garbage bags, spray, and rags downstairs.

"Let's start," Jay said, rubbing his hands together.

We took down the old saris, dupattas, bats, and scary stuff we had put up. Kavita gathered all the garbage and put it in a plastic bag.

Now there were only boxes left. Most of the boxes were decorated on the inside but not on the outside, except for Kavita's ladybug.

"How did our haunted tunnel turn into brown boxes?" Kavita asked.

"Into *stinky* boxes," I said when I lifted up one.

Jay covered his nose. "What's that smell coming from?"

Kavita pointed at the box I was holding. "From that?"

I dropped the box. "Looks like James threw up."

"How do you know it was James?" Jay asked.

"Because he covered his mouth when he came out of the tunnel the second time."

"And then he ran home," Kavita said.

"It was good that he was the last one through," Jay said.

"I thought James covered his nose and mouth because

he didn't like the smell of smooshed rice. I wondered if he ate a big lunch," I said.

Jay nodded. "Crawling through a haunted tunnel on a full stomach is a bad idea."

"Good thing Mrs. Crump didn't go through our stinky tunnel," Kavita said.

"Yes, that would have been really, really embarrassing. Now how are we going to fold that box? I don't want to touch it again. Any ideas, Jay?" I turned around. "Jay? Where did he disappear to?"

"Disappear? He must be magical," Kavita said.

I wondered if Jay had fled because of the smell. I plopped onto the bottom step. "I don't know how to take care of all this!"

Kavita sat down by me. "Let's do it tomorrow."

There was a big danger in not cleaning up now.

The not-cleaning-up danger list

∗ | The smell of that box was going to get

worse. Barf stinks. So old barf must stink ten times as bad as fresh barf.

* Other things were going to start smelling. Things like fake buttermilk blood and the fake grape eyeballs.

* Mom and Dad wouldn't be happy with a stinking basement.

* Stinky or more stinky, eventually, we would have to clean it up.

* If we don't, Mom and Dad would never allow us to build a haunted tunnel again.

* My head was really tired.

I grabbed my head so I could think better. I don't know if grabbing your head helps you think better or not, but it does keep it from spinning.

Jay returned with a large trash bag, like the one we use

to collect leaves. He also had three pairs of latex gloves, like the one I'd used to make the bloody hand.

"That's perfect. I'll get a container of wipes," I said. "Thanks so much for your help, Jay."

"Did you think I ran away?"

"Maybe."

He smiled.

We each put on a pair of gloves. Then we flattened the box, trying not to breathe. It wasn't easy, but we did it.

"I'll hold the bag open so you two can slide the box into it," Jay said.

When we were done, he tied off the bag and took it upstairs and outside to the trash can. The basement didn't smell good, but it didn't smell as bad.

After that the cleaning went fast. We sprayed and wiped the floor and tossed the rags in the garbage. I like recycling but not the stinky rags.

When we had gathered all the rest of the trash and recycling, I went upstairs and got a box of baking soda, sprinkled it on the floor, and vacuumed up the area. Then we washed up.

It was not even five when we finished.

In-my-head-list of why our cleanup had gone so fast
✳ I think things go three times as fast when three people are working on the same project.
✳ It's more fun when you are working with your sister and best friend. (And fun always goes fast)
✳ Especially when you don't argue and you work together as a team.

I had promised Mom and Dad that we'd clean up, so I asked them to come downstairs and see if there was a speck of dirt left.

"This looks so clean," Dad said.

"Even cleaner than before, because all the boxes are gone," Mom said.

I handed Mom five dollars from the money we'd collected.

"You took care of all of the boxes and cleaned up so well," she said. "I'll cover the cider expenses."

I was so happy. "Jay, Kavita, let's go upstairs and count the money!"

"Count the money?" Kavita's eyes widened, as if she had never seen money before. I guess this was the first time she was going to see money going from my hand to hers.

I emptied my pockets and put the money on the dining table. "That's like a thousand dollars! We're rich," Kavita said.

"Not really. It's just a bunch of dollar bills and some change. Do you want to count it?" I asked her.

While Kavita smoothed out the bills, she sang, "*Money, money, money, I will buy some honey. Honey, honey, honey, I love honey more than money.*"

Jay and I had some apple cider.

"Thanks for staying," I said.

"Thanks for letting Jeff go for free."

I wanted to tell Jay that Jeff had paid, but Jeff had told me not to tell.

"What is it?" Jay asked.

"Nothing," I said.

"There is something. I can tell," Jay said. His eyes got all squinty and narrow as he tried to figure out the secret.

Jay was my best friend. I didn't want to hide anything from him. Plus, I had not promised Jeff that I would keep this a secret.

"Jeff paid," I said.

"Oh, that's good," Jay said.

"Were you upset when you thought that he got in for free?"

"No." He shrugged. "I don't care."

"That's what I thought."

"We made twenty-four dollars and three quarters!" Kavita hollered.

"Three quarters is seventy-five cents," I said. "How did we get three quarters?"

"I think a quarter might have rolled away," Kavita said. "From your hand, Nina."

"Kavita, now you can buy lots of honey," Jay said.

"Honey is too sticky," Kavita said. "I don't like it."

"Then why were you singing about liking honey?" Jay glanced at me.

"Because it rhymes with 'money.' Singing is all about rhyming and I like singing, even if I don't like honey."

"O...kay," Jay said.

"Honey, money, I don't care," I said. "Jay, thanks for all your help. With everything. It was so much more fun because you were here." I offered Jay and Kavita some of the chocolate cookies that Mrs. Crump had brought.

"Thanks!" Jay took one. "The whole afternoon was super fun!"

"Not for James." Kavita said.

"I guess not." Jay sat down next to Kavita. "You each made more than twelve dollars. Not bad."

"We should divide the money three ways, so we'll each have eight dollars and twenty-five cents," I said.

"Three ways?" Kavita asked.

I crossed my fingers for luck before I said, "Yes, between you, Jay, and me." I hoped Kavita would want to share with Jay too.

Kavita was quiet while she chewed.

Jay said, "It's OK. You worked hard on building the tunnel."

Kavita wiped her hands on a paper towel. She picked up Jay's crown and placed it on his head. "King Yama also worked hard."

I gave Jay his share of the money. He looked shocked. Not shocked like he had gulped a live fish but like someone had given him a free ride on a carousel. It made me feel like I was getting a free ride on a carousel too.

"It's almost five fifteen," Jay said. "I have to go. See you soon."

"Have fun with Jeff," Kavita said as Jay zipped up his jacket.

"What? Aren't you guys coming with us for trick or treating?"

Now it was my turn to be shocked. "Aren't you going with Jeff?"

"So? He can come with us, right? We always go together. That's the tradition." He opened the door. "The tunnel was awesome fun."

Now I was ready for some real treats. We had some of Mrs. Crump's cookies, so I guess we had already started. And Kavita, Jay, and I had had enough cider already.

Kavita put her butterfly costume on top of her rose bush and aphids clothes. It was magnificent.

Mag-nif-i-cent means something that is so great that you almost can't believe it's true.

The middle of the monarch butterfly was painted on her shirt and the wings were attached to her shoulders. When Kavita opened her arms, the black and orange butterfly came alive.

I wore my velvet robe on top of my black leotard and pants. That way I was toasty warm. Then Mom fastened the tiara on my head.

When we were almost ready to go out, the doorbell rang. I took the bowl of candy and opened the door. King Yama and T. Rex—I mean, Jay and Jeff—stood there.

"Want to go trick or treat with us?" Jeff asked.

Jay didn't say anything and with his mask I couldn't see his expression. But his eyes sparkled.

"Sure." I held out the bowl of candy. "Take your treats first."

As I went out trick or treating with my sister, my best friend, and his cousin, I made an in-my-head list of everything that had worked out so beautifully.

* Our haunted tunnel had turned out to be more awesome than I had imagined.
* So many visitors had loved it.
* Even King Yama—I mean Jay—had helped.
* We had made money and it felt good to have shared it with Jay.
* Also, dividing twenty-four dollars and seventy-five cents three ways had worked out perfectly. We even got lucky that a quarter had rolled away.
* Now Jeff felt like my sort-of, kind-of friend too.
* We were going to get tons of candy.
* I was lucky with Halloween.

Even though I was not really the Halloween Queen of a haunted palace, it was OK. I had enjoyed being the Ladybug Queen of a haunted tunnel.

Now I was double queen because I was wearing one queen costume on top of another.

***

Kavita and I came home with a large bag full of candies. We each only ate one piece, because Mom and Dad said we couldn't have more that evening, especially after the cookies.

When I went to bed that night, I felt kind of happy and kind of sad that Halloween was over.

Until next year.

Maybe I could start planning for even bigger, better project. I mean I had a whole entire year—if I didn't forget. Kavita and Jay could help me. Maybe even Jeff? I should write down all our plans in Sakhi.

Tomorrow was a school day and I had to go to sleep now. Maybe I could take one of the candies for a lunch treat.

Queen lucky!